The stories in this collection were previously published individually by
Candlewick Press, 2067 Massachusetts Avenue, Cambridge, MA 02140

First published by Walker Books Ltd.
87 Vauxhall Walk, London SE11 5HJ

Based on the Audio Visual series "Maisy." A King Rollo Films production for
Universal Pictures International Visual Programming. Original scripts by Andrew Brenner and Jeanne Willis.
Illustrated in the style of Lucy Cousins by King Rollo Films Ltd.

First edition in this form 2002

This edition published specially for Borders, Inc. 2002 by Candlewick Press

2 4 6 8 10 9 7 5 3 1

Printed in Hong Kong

This book was typeset in Lucy Cousins.
The illustrations were done in gouache.

Candlewick Press
2067 Massachusetts Avenue
Cambridge, Massachusetts 02140

visit us at www.candlewick.com

At Home with Maisy

Lucy Cousins

CANDLEWICK PRESS
CAMBRIDGE, MASSACHUSETTS

Maisy Makes Gingerbread

Maisy is in her
kitchen today.

She is going to
make gingerbread
cookies.

Maisy needs flour,
sugar, butter, eggs,
and ginger.

Maisy mixes
everything
together.

FLOUR

She rolls out the dough and cuts out different shapes.

Maisy puts
the cookies
into the oven.

Maisy licks the
bowl while the
cookies are baking.

Then she washes up.
Ding, Dong!
That's the doorbell!
Who can it be?

It's Charley and Tallulah!

Just in time for an afternoon snack.

Yum, Yum.
Nice gingerbread
cookies, Maisy.

Doctor Maisy

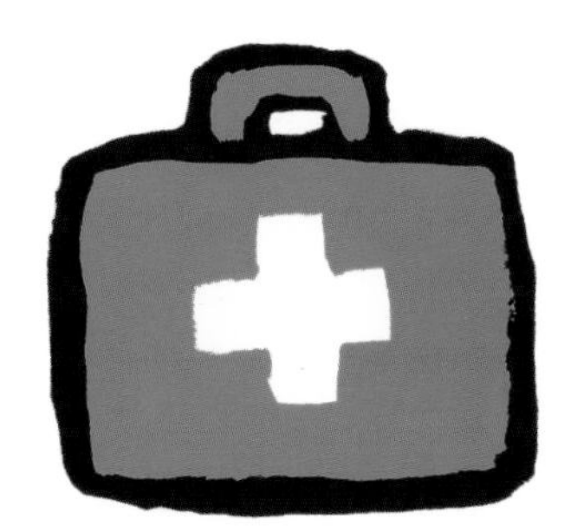

Hello, Doctor Maisy.
Hello, Nurse Tallulah.
Let's play hospital!

Tallulah listens to Maisy's heartbeat. That tickles!

Panda is sick today.
Maisy listens to
his heartbeat.
Thump, thump,
thump!

Maisy takes Panda's temperature.

Oh, no.
Panda has a fever.

Panda needs to rest.
Maisy carries him
up the stairs.

Night-night, Panda.
Get well soon.

Tallulah calls
from downstairs.
Maisy! Maisy!

Maisy runs
down the stairs.
Careful,
not too fast!

Crash!

Maisy bumps
into Tallulah.

Ouch!

Tallulah wraps
Maisy's nose
in a bandage.

That's better!
Bye-bye, Nurse Tallulah.
Bye-bye, Doctor Maisy.

Maisy Takes a Bath

It's Maisy's bathtime.

She runs the water and puts in some bubbles...

and in goes Duck.

Ding, Dong!
Oh, that's
the doorbell.

Maisy runs
downstairs to
see who it is.

Hello, Tallulah.

Maisy can't play now. It's her bathtime.

Maisy runs back upstairs and gets undressed.

Maisy jumps into
the bubbly bath.

Ding, Dong!
Who is ringing the
doorbell now?

Hello again, Tallulah!

Maisy is still taking her bath. Come and play later.

Oh! Where are you going, Tallulah?

Tallulah runs up
to the bathroom
and takes off
her clothes.

Splash, splash!

Maisy and Tallulah
play in the bath.

Hooray!

Maisy's Bedtime

Maisy is sleepy.
It's time for bed.
It's bedtime for
Panda, too.

Maisy closes
her bedroom
curtains.

Tuwhoo, tuwhoo,
hoots the owl.

Maisy washes her
face and brushes
her teeth.

Maisy puts on
her pajamas.

Maisy gets
into bed and
reads a story.

But where
is Panda?

Is he in the
toy box?

Oh, there he is!

Maisy turns
off the light.

But she still
isn't ready to
go to sleep.

Maisy forgot to
use the toilet!

Panda sits on
his potty, too.

Maisy is very sleepy now.

Good night, Maisy.
Good night, Panda.